THE EMIGRANT DOCTOR IN THE DEATH BOAT

THE EMIGRANT DOCTOR IN THE DEATH BOAT

ALI TOBI

PARTRIDGE

To order additional copies of this book, contact
Toll Free 800 101 2657 (Singapore)
Toll Free 1 800 81 7340 (Malaysia)
orders.singapore@partridgepublishing.com

www.partridgepublishing.com/singapore

Labib Mansour stood at the seaport in Gambia, saying good-bye to his wife Salma and his ten-year-old son, Khalil.

"I want you to promise us that you will take care of yourself and come back to us safely," Salma said.

"I promise you, and *Inshaa Allah* (if God wishes), I'll do my best to survive this journey and come back to you with a lot of money. Then we will start a new life full of happiness," Labib replied.

"Please don't go, Dad. We need you here!" Khalil begged.

"I'm doing this for you, son. When I come back, I'll send you to a good school. You will have good clothes and eat excellent food."

Khalil asked, "Who will take care of us when you go?"

"You are a man now. Just listen to your mom and support her. I'm depending on you until I get back."

"Try to make your trip short, and don't stay there any longer than you have to," Salma said.

"I hope two years will be long enough to make good money," Labib said.

Salma smiled sadly. "We will miss you."

"I will miss you too. Take care of yourselves. I have to go now. The ship is about to sail."

Labib met some new African friends on board the ship, and all of them had prepared themselves for the illegal entry into Spain to search for new lives.

"Welcome on board, everyone. I wish you a safe and happy journey. I am also hoping you are fit and good swimmers too," the captain said. "Not all of you will survive this trip. Whoever feels that he can't make it for any reason still has a chance to get off the ship now and go back to his family. I don't want to be responsible for your death."

"To remain here is also death," someone replied.

The captain asked, "Does that mean you are all ready for this dangerous journey?"

"Yes!" everyone shouted.

"Let us move then."

A week later, in the middle of the sea at night, the captain ordered the crew to lower three small boats into the water. "This is the end of my trip with you. I wish you a good new life."

"What do you mean?" Labib asked.

"We have put out three boats for three groups of you to continue your trip without us."

"But the boats are too small, and we are many!" someone shouted.

"You have no choice now," the captain said. "Either come back with me or get into the boats and sail away."

"How long do you think it will take us to reach land?" Labib asked.

"About ten days," the captain answered.

"Please, can you get closer to land?" one of the immigrants asked.

The captain replied, "If I do that, the police will catch me."

"Okay. Don't move until we organize ourselves in the boats," Saleh said.

"One boat is completely full," Edward said. "Others can go to the second one."

"Hurry up, guys. Let's get into this boat," Labib said.

"We have to squeeze ourselves. There isn't enough space," Edward said.

"Have you finished? I need to go. Don't forget to bring me gifts when you get back from Spain," the captain joked.

At nighttime most of the immigrants were sleeping.

"Shark! A shark is attacking the other boat!" Saleh shouted.

Edward cried loudly, "Be careful, guys. He is coming to us."

"I am hitting him with a big stick," Labib said.

"I'll also use a knife to scare him," Saleh said.

The shark managed to sink one of the boats and kill some of the immigrants. Then it went away.

"Help! Help!" someone shouted.

"Wait! Wait! I'm coming to you." Labib swam and rescued him.

Edward told one of the survivors, "Catch the rope. I'll pull you up to the boat."

"We have to squeeze ourselves again in two boats and make space for other passengers," Saleh said.

"We are hungry, thirsty, and tired," some of the immigrants cried.

Seven days later, one of the immigrants shouted, "Land! Land!"

"Oh my God! Unfortunately one more died before we reached land," Edward said sadly.

The police knew about the immigrant boats.

"I have asked the police ships to lead the boats with the immigrants into the port," the colonel said.

"Any idea how many there are?" the major general asked.

"There might be five hundred immigrants. We have called the ambulances for help."

The major general was amazed. "What? Do you want to treat them also? Isn't it enough we are going to feed them? They have entered the country illegally. Cancel the ambulances."

"But ... but," the colonel stammered.

"There is no but here. I'm in charge, and this is an order. If there is any doctor on duty at the port, tell him to go home."

"Yes, sir, I'll do that."

In a few hours, the boats carrying the immigrants, very weak from hunger, thirst, and exposure, were escorted into the port.

"Don't you know that what have you done is illegal and you will go straight to jail?" the major general asked. "Look at you, so tired, hungry, and dying."

The immigrants were standing, and one fainted. Labib moved to help him.

But the major general beat him and then said, "Don't move until I allow you. What have you heard about us? Do we provide food and medicine for free? We are not a charity organization. You have to work to be paid, and you must do that legally. I have been talking to you for a half hour. Is there anyone who understands what I am saying? Does anyone speak Spanish or English?"

While the major general was talking, his voice started to weaken, and he started sweating and couldn't stand anymore. He fell down unconscious.

The colonel shouted, "Somebody call the ambulance or a doctor!"

"Unfortunately we have asked the doctor to go home, as we were instructed to do," one of the police officers said.

"Can someone bring milk or water? I know he is diabetic. The milk will make him feel better," the colonel ordered.

Soon somebody gave him milk, but he couldn't open his mouth or eyes.

Labib stepped forward. "He is in serious condition because, besides the diabetes, he also has a heart problem. I'm a doctor. I can check him until the ambulance arrives. We have no time to lose. He may die if we delay."

"Are you sure about this?" the colonel asked. "Come and help?"

Labib started cardiopulmonary resuscitation until the major general opened his eyes. He tried to talk but was unable to. An hour later the ambulance arrived and took the major general to the hospital.

"Because you have saved his life," the colonel told Labib, "I'll arrange for some food and medicine."

The immigrants shouted, "Dr. Labib! Dr. Labib!"

The colonel sent all the immigrants to jail.

"Man, you didn't tell us you were a doctor! Is that true?" Saleh was surprised.

"I am so sorry I couldn't save anyone at sea," Labib said sadly. "This hurts me a lot."

"That was out of your hands. As far as I know, no one died because of disease," Saleh said. "They all died because of hunger, thirst, and drowning."

"You also can speak English," Edward said. "That will help us to understand them."

"It is now time to sleep," said one of the jail guards as he turned off the lights.

In the morning all the prisoners were standing in the yard.

"I want all of you to follow the rules of this jail. You will be punished if you break them. I'm expecting you to keep order. One of you who speaks English must explain to the others," Kevin, the jail officer, said.

Labib translated to the others what Kevin said.

"I don't know if they will allow us to call our families," Edward said.

"Will they allow us to work here?" Saleh asked.

Labib said, "If they are going to send us to court, we will have a lawyer and know our rights."

Five days later Tony, one of the prisoners, fell down the stairs and injured his head, which started to bleed. Immediately the jail doctor was there to help.

"Can you breathe? Don't move. You have fractured your head, and there might be internal bleeding," the doctor said.

"My stomach hurts," Tony cried.

"There is no injury to your stomach," the doctor said.

Labib and his friends were watching.

"My stomach. My stomach!"

"I am telling you. Nothing is wrong with your stomach. Don't you understand?"

"Please, Doctor," Labib asked. "Can I say something?"

"Can't you see that I am busy with the patient?" the doctor replied.

"I am a doctor, too, and I can help," Labib said.

The doctor snapped, "I am in charge here, not you."

"Excuse me, Doctor. If Tony is not operated on urgently, he might die," Labib said.

"Are you teaching me my job? I know what I'm doing. I'm checking if there is internal bleeding. And you'd better keep quiet before I tell security to punish you," the angry doctor said.

"I don't care what you are going to do to me," Labib said. "I'm concerned about Tony's life. He is trying to tell you that the pain in the stomach is more than in his head, and I'm afraid it is appendicitis. I can see symptoms of the disease, which might cause death if someone does not operate on him soon."

The doctor checked Tony's stomach and found it was appendicitis, meaning he was in need of an urgent operation. Soon the ambulance arrived.

The guard was watching. "Now we have two doctors in the jail!"

"You must be paid, Dr. Labib," Saleh joked.

Labib smiled. "It is prayer time. Let's go."

The next morning the guard said, "You have a visitor, Labib."

"Who could it be? I have no friends in this country," Labib said.

"I'll go and have some coffee," the jail officer said.

The major general came to see Labib.

"Good to see you well, sir," Labib said.

"I just came to say thank you for saving my life," the major general said. "The doctor in the hospital said I was lucky because I had only a few minutes to survive if I did not get the medical attention I required. I can't imagine what would have happened if you were not there. I would like also to apologize for beating you."

"The most important thing is that you are fine and can continue with your job," Labib said.

"I have asked the jail officer to give you special treatment. And I'm looking for a good lawyer to defend you. If you need anything else, please let me know," the major general said.

"Thank you. That is kind of you, sir."

"I have to go now," the major general said.

Labib was so glad about what he heard.

Once he was back in the jail, Edward asked, "What happened? Are they going to release us?"

"They are going to send us to court for trial," Labib said.

Saleh said, "I hope they will get us a good lawyer who can support our case."

Labib said, "That is what the major general promised me that he would do."

"Are you telling us he was the visitor?" Edward asked.

"Yes, he was."

"I was not expecting to get help from him," Saleh said. "What a big change!"

The guard interrupted, "Labib, you have another visitor in the same office."

"I am going to have more coffee," the jail officer said.

"Hi, Labib. My name is Bob Robinson. I am here to thank you for helping my son."

"Who is your son, sir?"

"Sorry. My son is Tony. Yesterday you diagnosed my son with appendicitis."

"How is he now?" Labib asked.

"He is doing well. Can you please stay close to my son? I'll pay you. Don't worry. I'm rich and can afford it," Bob said.

"I don't mind helping anyone, as that is my job as a doctor."

"I can depend on you," Bob said.

"Don't worry as long I'm here," Labib said. "I'll take care of him."

"Time is up," interrupted the jail officer.

"I am leaving. Thank you and see you soon," Bob said.

"Wait, Labib. Don't go. I want to talk to you," the jail officer said.

"Yes, sir. I'm listening."

"I heard a lot about you. I was just wondering what someone like you is doing here."

"I'm looking for a better life, sir."

"Do you treat all diseases?"

"No, sir, but I do my best."

"See this photo? She is my nine-year-old daughter Kathy. She has been sick for five years."

"What is wrong with her?" Labib asked.

"The problem is that even the doctors don't know what is making her sick," the jail officer explained. "We have visited many doctors and good hospitals locally and overseas. They prescribe painkillers only. I don't know what to do."

"That means she's been sick since she was four years old," Labib said.

"I don't know why I'm telling you all this."

"Can you please call your daughter and let me talk to her?" Labib asked.

"Are you going to treat her over the phone?"

"No, sir, but normally doctors ask questions before giving a diagnosis and medication."

The jail officer called Kathy on the phone. "I have a doctor in front of me. He wants to ask you some questions."

"Okay, Dad."

"Hi, Kathy. My name is Labib. Can I ask about your illness?"

"Please do," Kathy replied.

"Where do you feel the pain? And do you have it all the time?"

"The pain is in my stomach, and the only time I don't feel it is early morning before breakfast."

"Thank you. That is all I wanted to ask."

"Bye, Kathy. See you at home," the jail officer said.

"I'm not sure, but maybe I can do something for her," Labib said.

"Just a few questions and you already know what is causing the pain?" The jail officer was surprised.

"That is my job, sir."

Once the jail officer was at home, his wife Liza said, "Dinner is ready, Kevin."

"I am starving. What is there on the table?" Kevin asked.

"Everything is homemade."

"Mmm. Delicious."

"What about you, Kathy?" Liza asked.

"I'd like more bread, please."

"The weekend is coming. Any plans?" Kevin asked.

Kathy said, "I don't feel like I want to go anywhere."

"No problem. Maybe we can go somewhere next weekend," Liza said.

"Yah. It was good. Thank you," Kathy said. "Excuse me. I'm going to finish my school homework."

"Don't forget to take your medicine, honey," Liza said.

Kevin said, "I want to talk to you about something, Liza."

"Go ahead, darling. I'm listening."

"I have a prisoner who talked to Kathy on the phone, and he thinks can treat her."

"Good doctors and hospitals have failed to identify the

problem with our daughter, and you think a prisoner can help?"

"Not only is he a prisoner, he's a doctor as well. He saved the lives of Bob's son and the major general."

"Why is he in jail?"

"He entered the country illegally."

"So what are you thinking about?" Liza asked.

"I am thinking of smuggling him out of the jail and then sending him back after treating our daughter."

"No. No. That is not a good idea. I don't want you to risk yourself and future just for an illegal immigrant to cheat us."

"That was not his suggestion. It is mine," Kevin strongly said.

"Wait, Kevin. We will go to see another doctor."

"We have tried so many hospitals. Now the time has come for a change."

"Think about this carefully before making any quick decisions," Liza said.

"This is the only chance we have. I can't bear to see my

daughter suffering this way anymore," Kevin said, ending the conversation.

In the jail, Edward asked, "When are they going to allow us to talk to our families?"

Labib said, "I hope soon."

"We haven't seen a lawyer yet," Saleh said.

Tony interrupted, "Hi! Can I join you guys?"

"How do you feel now?" Labib asked.

"I am fine. Thank you for saving my life." Then he asked, "When are you going to be released?"

"We don't know yet," Saleh said.

"I have seen immigrants being sent to trial, and soon after that, they were sent back to their countries," Tony said.

Edward asked, "What about you? What is your case?"

"I killed someone while driving a car. I was under the influence of alcohol."

"How long is your judgment period?" Saleh asked.

"Eight years. I have already served three," Tony said. "My father is trying to pay blood money to the victim's family, and then I will be released."

Kevin called one of his security assistants.

"Yes, sir. What I can do for you?" Richard, the security in charge, replied.

"Please sit down, Richard. I have called you because I trust you more than anyone else here and we have been working together for many years."

"You can always trust me," Richard said.

"I need your personal help. I know it is not easy, but you are the only one who can do the job."

"Do you have financial problems?" Richard asked. "Do you need some money?"

"No, it is not about that. You are aware of my daughter's illness. All the doctors we have gone to see have not been able to diagnose what is wrong with her."

"I know that," Richard said.

"I think I have the right doctor who can treat my daughter."

"That is good news. What are you waiting for? Take her to see the doctor."

"The problem is that the doctor is in this jail."

"Do you mean Labib?" Richard was surprised.

"Yes, he is!"

"So what are you thinking of doing?" Richard asked.

"If you will help me, we can smuggle him out of the prison just to see Kathy. Then we will bring him back," Kevin said.

"That is very dangerous. If we are caught, we will end up in jail. Please think of another solution," Richard said.

"I am not forcing you. We can make a plan without anybody else noticing. Please go home and think of my daughter who is in so much pain every day and praying for a cure."

The guard opened the jail door for the lawyer to see the immigrants.

"Hi, Labib. I am your lawyer. My name is Chris Fraser. In ten days you will be going on trial for entering this country illegally. I guess you are going to represent all the other immigrants."

"What do you think the judge is going to decide?" Labib asked.

"Can't say. The government is so strict nowadays about illegal immigrants, and of course that will reflect in the decision of the court."

"So things are going to get worse." Labib was disappointed.

"I have to go. I may visit you before court if necessary," the lawyer said.

Two days later Richard entered Kevin's office. "How do we know if Labib won't escape?"

"I'll be watching him," Kevin answered.

"How many nights will he be away?" Richard asked.

"Just three days."

"What is the plan?" Richard asked.

"Thanks, Richard. I know you won't let me down. We'll tell the internal guard that Labib is going to another jail for a few days. Then he will be back. You are in charge, and he has no right to question you. The outside gate is the main problem."

"So what are you going to do about that?" Richard asked.

"I have a spare police uniform and a fake police ID card. I'll request a van, and Labib can change into the police uniform in the van. And once we get to the gate, the security will open the van door but see two police officers, you and Labib, sitting. And of course masks will cover your faces, as you have an undercover mission."

"It looks good. But what about bringing him back?" Richard asked.

"We will follow the same plan on the way back. Just after we pass the police gate, Labib will take off the police uniform and wear the prisoner uniform," Kevin said reliably.

"When are we going to start?" Richard asked.

"Tonight is fine."

"I am ready to help your daughter," Richard said.

"Don't worry, Richard. Everything will be all right," Kevin said.

Kevin sent the guard to call Labib.

"Sir, you called me?" Labib asked.

"Are three days enough for you to treat my daughter?"

"I will do my best, sir," Labib said.

"I want you to keep this a secret. Don't tell your friends. Tonight we will take you out from the jail undercover," Kevin said.

"Why undercover?" Labib asked. "Is that the legal way to do it?"

"The court doesn't allow us to do it legally," Kevin said. "We have no choice and no time."

"What am I supposed to tell my friends?" Labib asked.

"Tell them you are being moved to another jail for a couple days and then you will be back."

"Please listen to me, dear friends. I'm being moved to another jail for a few days. Then I'll be back," Labib said.

"What are we going to do if they won't allow you to come back?" Edward asked.

"I don't trust them either," Saleh said. "Until today they have not allowed us to call our families."

"Don't worry, friends. I promise you that I'll be back soon."

"Bring Labib to the jail officer," Richard asked the guard.

"Don't stay there longer. Our jail has five-star standards," the guard joked to Labib.

"You can go," Kevin asked the guard.

"I am going to arrange the van," Richard said.

Labib asked, "Are you scared, sir?"

"I am not afraid of myself, but for Richard in case anything goes wrong," Kevin replied.

"Let's hope that everything will go well," Labib said.

The van arrived at an outside gate.

The gate guard asked Kevin, "How many of you are going, sir?"

"We total three with two in the back," Kevin answered.

"Can I see them, please?"

"Sure you can."

"Do you have a mission outside, guys?" the guard asked.

"Yes, sir," both Richard and Labib replied.

"Be careful, guys,"

"Okay. Open the gate."

"We made it. We are out!" Kevin shouted.

"What happens now?" Richard asked.

"I have parked my personal car behind the trees. I'll go home with Labib."

"What about the van? I'm not allowed to take it home," Richard asked.

"Because we can't park this van here, please take it to the police garage. Tell them something is wrong with it and it needs to be repaired," Kevin said.

"I wonder if you have missed anything in the plan."

Kevin arrived home. "This is Dr. Labib, and this is my wife, Liza."

"Nice meeting you," Liza welcomed him.

"Good meeting you too, madam."

"And here is my lovely daughter, Kathy."

"Hi, Kathy. Do you remember me?"

"Yes, I spoke to you a few days ago," Kathy said.

"Dr. Labib will be with us for some time. He will try to treat you," Kevin said.

"But where is his medical bag? Normally all doctors carry one," Kathy asked.

"I have forgotten it in my car, but never mind. Your father will arrange one."

"Can we eat something, guys?" Liza suggested.

"No, madam. Please, I'll be the cook from now onwards," Labib said.

"What?" Liza was surprised.

"Sorry, I'm not sure, but I think something in the food is causing your daughter's illness, and I am here to find out what it is."

"Good start," Kevin said. "This is different than our experience with other doctors."

"Can you please show me the kitchen?" Labib asked.

"Let me take you," Kevin said.

"Fine. I also need a stethoscope, blood pressure machine, urine and blood sample bottles, and a syringe," Labib requested.

"I'll ask Liza to bring everything you need."

Labib was grouping the food into salty, sugar, oil, dairy, fish, meat, chicken, and so forth. He was taking notes and preparing the menus for breakfast, lunch, and dinner.

"So what is my dinner today?" Kathy asked.

"Fish and potatoes," Labib replied.

"I hope you are a good cook too," Kathy said.

"I want you to promise me please that you will not eat or drink anything without my permission," Labib said.

"I will obey your orders," Kathy said.

Labib was observing, monitoring, keeping notes, and watching Kathy's movements, and after two days there was little improvement. Then Richard visited Kevin's house.

"Hi, Richard."

"I just want to remind you, Kevin, that Labib is supposed to return to jail tomorrow."

"What do you think, Labib?" Kevin asked.

"I need three more days, please. I am about to complete my investigation and diagnosis."

"We are going to be in trouble," Richard said.

Liza said, "Please, Richard, give him another few days. Kathy is progressing well."

"Come on, Kevin. Say something. You promised me that you needed Labib for three days only."

"I am so sorry. My daughter is doing well. Labib should not stop now. Don't worry. Nothing will go wrong," Kevin said.

"If I lose my job, I won't forgive you, Kevin."

"Thank you so much. The plan is going well so far," Kevin said.

"Just three days and no more," Richard said.

"Shall I make some coffee for you?" Liza asked.

"No thanks. I have to go now."

The next morning, while Labib and Kathy were outside the house, a police officer came.

"I haven't seen you in a long time, Frank. Welcome to my house," Kevin said with fear.

"Yes, it is. Actually I'm here for work. It has been reported that a prisoner has escaped and is in this area."

"Who could it be?" Kevin asked.

"A car robber," Frank replied.

Kevin thanked God.

Once Labib saw the police officer, he immediately pretended to be exercising and waved to him.

"Strange. Is he your guest?" Frank asked. "He is exercising without wearing the proper attire!"

"It does not matter to him what he is wearing. As soon as he decided to exercise, nothing could stop him. What a strange man!" Kevin replied.

"Just tell your guest to report to us if he sees the robber and tell him to wear proper gear for running," Frank joked.

"Of course I'll tell him."

"Take care and see you," Frank said.

"Keep in touch."

"Dad, why is the doctor suddenly doing exercises?" Kathy asked.

"That is because he is a smart doctor."

"Is Richard gone?" Liza asked.

"That was not him. It was Frank."

"Oh my God! I hope he didn't notice anything."

"Has he gone?" Labib asked.

"Thank you, Doctor," Kevin said. "That was a good idea. I like it."

Labib said, "I have good news for you. I have finished my job."

"Great! It is one day before the deadline," Kevin said.

"Are you sure she is going to be fine, Doctor?" Liza asked.

"As I told you earlier, the problem is in the food."

"Let's go inside and talk more," Kevin said.

"Your daughter has a wheat allergy. She should stop eating or drinking anything that contains gluten. It causes her to lose weight and makes her tired and weak. It causes cramps in the stomach. If she is not going to be treated properly, it will also cause anemia, kidney stones, and colon, heart, and urine problems. Instead of wheat, she can eat corn or rice flour, and the benefits are the same as wheat except they do not contain gluten. Please go to the hospital and tell them your daughter has celiac disease."

"Why have doctors failed to diagnose this problem?" Kevin asked.

"Celiac is a very rare disease, and it is not easy to diagnose. Some doctors think it is diarrhea or stomach pain. It is important to do the right medical tests."

"Can this be treated?" Liza asked.

"Actually the treatment is easier than the diagnosis."

Kevin asked, "How long will it take for her to recover?"

"If Kathy avoids wheat products and takes the proper medication, she will see the improvement in only a few weeks."

"I can't believe it," Liza said sadly. "All these years I have been feeding my daughter food that she is allergic to."

"Now can I go back to the prison before you get into trouble?"

Kevin and Liza were very quiet. They didn't know what to say.

"While you are discussing, can I have your phone? I'll tell Kathy to call your friend Richard," Labib said.

Richard arrived at Kevin's house. "Yes, Kevin. You called me?"

"Be ready tonight. We are taking Labib back to the jail."

"That is good news, but has he succeeded? And where is Labib now? That window is open," Richard said.

All of them were afraid and thought Labib had run away. Suddenly they found him reading a book in the library.

"I am here. I didn't escape. I'm sorry. I saw the door to the library was open."

"It is fine. You can read the books," Kevin said.

"Now I'm taking her to the hospital," Liza said. "I would

like to thank you for everything you have done for my daughter. I wish the court will release you, let you stay in the country, and share your experience with other doctors."

Kathy asked, "Will I see you again?"

"That depends on your country."

"I will prepare the van," Richard said.

On their way to the jail, Kevin said, "The plan will be the same as when we left the prison. Labib wears the police uniform and a face mask, and once we pass through the gate and before he leaves the van, he will change into the prison uniform."

The van arrived at the gate.

"Can I see your pass, please?" the gate guard asked.

"Here it is." Kevin showed him.

"Open the van and let them take off their masks," the gate guard ordered.

When Labib heard the guard coming toward him, he pretended to have an epileptic fit and cried loudly.

"We have to take him urgently to the doctor. He needs an injection," Richard said.

"Guard, are you coming with us?" Kevin asked.

"Just go," the guard said. "I hope he is going to be fine."

"That was another good trick, Labib," Kevin joked. "I hope you really don't have epilepsy."

Labib immediately wore the prison uniform, and as he was getting out of the van, the other prisoners saw him and welcomed him back.

"How was the other jail?" someone shouted.

"See you soon, guys," Labib answered them.

In his office, Kevin said, "I would like to thank both of you for your help. Without you, this plan wouldn't have worked."

"You are most welcome, sir," Labib said.

Richard said, "Thank God everything went well."

"Can I see my friends in the jail? I have missed them."

"Yes, you can."

The phone rang.

Kevin answered, "Hi, Liza. What did the doctor say?"

"You won't believe it. The doctor said exactly what Labib said, and then we went to see another one and confirmed that Kathy has celiac disease."

"Why was the disease so hard to diagnose?" Kevin asked.

"It is over now, Kevin. Our daughter is going to be fine."

"I hope so. I hope so."

In the jail, Saleh said, "Thank you for coming back, Doctor Labib."

Edward said, "I hope they treated you well."

"The jail and people were good," Labib said. "But I can't stay away from you."

"Any news about sending us to court?" Saleh asked.

"It is not much longer any more," Labib said.

"Let's hope we win the case," Edward said.

Kevin met the lawyer, major general, and Bob Robinson.

"The case will go to court the day after tomorrow," the lawyer said.

Kevin asked, "Have you prepared for it?"

"Of course I have."

"We don't want to lose the case," the major general said.

"I am ready to pay more if required," Bob offered.

"Do you want to see the immigrants before the court?" Kevin asked the lawyer.

"There is no need. Please just inform them of the date."

On the day of the case, the judge said, "In front of me is a statement from the defense lawyer who wants the court to punish the illegal immigrants so no one will repeat it in the future. They want us to jail and repatriate them. Do you want to comment anything, Lawyer?"

"Thank you, Your Honor. Those immigrants are looking for your forgiveness and help, and they promise they will not do it again. Please let them stay for some time, and they can later return home. That's all I have to say, Your Honor."

"What about you, Labib? As you are representing the others, do you want to say something?" the judge asked.

"Thank you very much, Your Honor. It is my pleasure to talk to you, and I thank Allah we are still alive and able to stand in front of you after surviving death in crossing the ocean. My colleagues and I would like to apologize for entering your country illegally, but we did that because we had no choice. And someone should deliver the message to you from the African countries.

"If you will allow me, Your Honor, about three hundred years ago, your people forced our grandfathers to work in your farms and factories and treated them as slaves. And we never asked you to pay us back for that, and we also do remember colonization days.

"Today all we want from developed countries is to help us develop our poor countries. There are so many ways to do that if you are interested in providing for the health of our people, educating our children, and building roads, electricity plants, agriculture sectors, and so forth. Invest in our countries, open your market for our products, and provide us soft loans, technology, scholarship grants, and so forth. With your support and encouragement, our economy can improve a lot. In doing so, it will reflect positively in the West, and you will have no more illegal immigrants.

"The world has become a small village. Working together, we can control diseases and stop them from spreading and crossing borders. Are some people in your countries affected from the Ebola virus? In the hospital where I worked, there was shortage of all types of medicines and doctors too. I took the risk to send you this message too. We are also suffering from hunger and poverty. Please help us to stop all this suffering. Don't we deserve a better life?"

"This is my first time I feel someone is judging me," the judge said.

Labib continued talking, "Excuse me, Your Honor. We are not in a position to judge you. All we want from you is to think about us. Who are we? Where did we come from? Why are we in your country? What kind of people are we? Which life is better for us? Do we look like criminals or drug dealers? Aren't we human beings like you? Do you know how we made this trip, sire? We sold everything and spent a lot of money to make this journey happen. I can also say we sold our lives too!"

"Do you really need a lawyer, Labib?" the judge interrupted.

"Your Honor, we are looking for justice here. We have left our families behind with nothing. It is not fair to return to them with empty pockets. Your Honor, we do respect your decision and promise to follow the rules of this country and live in peace with your people."

"Will you please give us a chance to say something?" the judge asked.

The judge talked to his assistants. The court was silent for some time, waiting for the decision.

"Labib, as you are a doctor and you have saved the major general's and Tony Robinson's life, besides giving us a lecture on how developed countries can help poorer countries," the judge said, "we have decided to allow you to stay in the country and send the other illegal immigrants back to their countries."

"Please allow me to add something, Your Honor," Labib interrupted.

"What else, Labib?" the judge asked.

"With respect to your decision, Your Honor, just to let you know, the immigrants have chosen me to speak on their behalf. They encouraged me to treat and save people's lives. I am so sorry to tell you, Your Honor, but since I came with them, I'll go back with them," Labib said.

The judge banged the desk with the gavel. "Everyone, silent. Please let us meet after an hour."

"After discussions with my assistants, we have agreed to allow all illegal immigrants to stay in the country," the judge said. "Labib is allowed to go and bring his family to stay in the country for as long as he likes. The government will look into your request of helping and supporting the poorer African countries and will do the necessary things."

Everyone in the court was standing and clapping. Happy, they were hugging each other.

Labib brought his family, opened a clinic, and supplied medicines and other useful products to his country. Also the industrialized countries started giving more help to African countries in all areas of life.

Printed in the United States
By Bookmasters